The Bell Tolls at Mousehaven Manor

The Bell Tolls at Mousehaven Manor

by Mary DeBall Kwitz

illustrated by Stella Ormai

Scholastic Inc.
New York   Toronto   London   Auckland   Sydney

No part of this publication may be reproduced in whole or in part, or stored in a retrieval system, or transmitted in any form or by any means, electronic, mechanical, photocopying, or otherwise, without written permission of the publisher. For information regarding permission, write to Scholastic Inc., 555 Broadway, New York, NY 10012.

ISBN 0-590-43841-7

12 11 10 9 8 7   4 5 6 7 8/9

Printed in the U.S.A.   40

Wishing prairie-perfect days for
Suzanne and Karen

ॐ

Linda and Laurie

Contents

The Bell Tolls at Mousehaven Manor

When the prairie winds sigh:
"Stranger, stranger, stranger"
The tower bell will toll:
"Danger! Danger! Danger!"

— Percival M. Bat

1.

Company

"Company is coming," said Minabell Mouse, gazing out of Mousehaven Manor's parlor window. "Look, Aunt Pitty Pat." She pointed to a tiny speck silhouetted against the clouds.

With a tired little sigh, Aunt Pitty Pat Mouse got up from her rocker, rubbed her leg, and limped to the window. She searched the evening sky and saw a black spot moving slowly, growing larger as it came toward the manor. "Land sakes!" she said. "Our visitor is coming by prairie hawk."

"Are you sure it's a hawk, Aunt Pitty Pat?

Only someone coming from out of state would fly in on such a large bird."

Her aunt's eyes sparkled, and her side-whiskers twitched with excitement. "Oh, yes, mouseling! Prairie hawks have a special way of flying. They like to coast along, riding the air currents."

Minabell and her aunt had just that afternoon finished spring housecleaning. They were ready for company. The windows were washed, and floors scrubbed. And every piece of furniture in the stately old mansion was dusted, waxed, and polished.

Minabell glanced worriedly at Aunt Pitty Pat. Her aunt's whiskers had turned white, and the arthritis in her leg was painful. Minabell feared the spring cleaning had been too much for her. But her aunt had insisted on helping as usual. She enjoyed dusting, waxing, and window washing — almost as much as cooking.

Minabell put an arm around her aunt and looked out at the statue of Geronimouse, their famous ancestor. The statue stood on its stone pedestal in the center of Geronimouse Park surrounding the mansion. To the east loomed Indian Mound Hill. The visitor would be coming from that direction.

And moments later a large, brown bird appeared above the rim of the Hill. As he flew over Geronimouse, Minabell announced, "You're right, Aunt Pitty Pat. It's a hawk — and he's carrying a passenger."

They hurried outside and stood on the front steps, impatiently awaiting their guest.

The prairie hawk circled over the manor, loudly squawking his intention to land. Swooping down, the bird made a bumpy two-point landing in front of the manor. He dipped a wing to the ground so the passenger could get off.

A small, white mouse, twirling a lavender parasol, walked down the hawk's wing and daintily stepped onto the grass. She looked up at them through a fringe of dark lashes.

"Why, I do declare," she said in a soft Southern drawl, "if it isn't Cousin Minabell and Aunt Pitty Pat."

Aunt Pitty Pat stared at the pretty little creature. "Minabell, I believe it's Violet Mae!"

"Cousin Violet Mae?" cried Minabell, running down the steps, followed more slowly by her aunt.

"All the way from St. Augustine, Florida," said Violet Mae with a curtsy.

"Land sakes, child!" Aunt Pitty Pat held her at arm's length. "You're all grown up." She started to embrace her, but Violet Mae closed her parasol and handed it to Minabell.

Then she turned to Aunt Pitty Pat and allowed herself to be hugged.

"You must be tired and hungry from your journey," Aunt Pitty Pat said, guiding her up the steps.

Minabell followed, carrying the parasol.

"I'll show you to your bedroom, dear," her aunt continued as they entered the manor. "After you've freshened up, we'll have supper, and you can tell us the news from St. Augustine."

Aunt Pitty Pat turned to Minabell. "Percy is coming for supper tonight, too," she reminded her, with a happy little twitch of her side-whiskers. Minabell knew how much her aunt enjoyed parties, and tonight's supper was turning into a real dinner party.

"Percy Bat is our neighbor," said Aunt Pitty Pat, leading Cousin Violet Mae through the foyer, across the hall, and up the grand staircase. "He and his family live in the bell tower."

Minabell watched her cousin's elegant white tail disappear up the staircase. What good times we will have together, she thought happily. Aunt Pitty Pat loves company. This is just what she needs to brighten her spirits.

Minabell heard a loud flapping of wings outside the front door. "AHEM! Sorry, miss," called the prairie hawk. "I'll need help with the luggage."

Minabell looked out the door. For the first time, she noticed Violet Mae's luggage piled up high on the hawk's back. "Oh, dear! I'm sorry." She hurried back out and down the stairs.

Minabell quickly unloaded the luggage from the bird's back. Together they carried it into the foyer. The big bird looked at the pile of bags and boxes. "Sure glad to get rid of that load." He gave Minabell a sympathetic look. "Wouldn't be surprised if she's planning a long visit."

The prairie hawk lifted a wingtip in salute and started out the door. He stopped and stepped back inside. "I almost forgot. Are you Ms. Minabell Mouse?"

"Oh, yes, sir. Indeed, I am."

The hawk reached into his shoulder pouch and brought out a package wrapped in a piece of old burlap. "My instructions were to give this to you — personally." The prairie hawk set the heavy parcel on the floor.

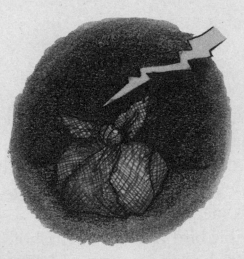

Minabell stared at it, aware of a sudden stillness in the foyer. A streak of lightning flashed outside the door. Blinded, she closed her eyes. A second later the silence was broken by a clap of the thunder that shook the windows. When she opened her eyes, the hawk was gone.

2.

The Mysterious Package

inabell ran outside. The hawk was just taking off.

"Wait, wait!" she shouted. "There's no name or address on the package. Are you sure it's meant for me?"

The big bird was out of earshot. Flapping his wings, he lifted up and over Geronimouse Park. Probably searching for a handy air current, thought Minabell. He'd better hurry before he's caught in the rainstorm.

But where was the storm? She looked up at the sky. Dusk had settled over the Illinois prairie. Stars glittered overhead, and a sliver of moon shone above Indian Mound Hill.

Not a hint of stormy weather. Strange. She was sure she had seen lightning and heard thunder.

Minabell went inside and closed the door, and her eyes strayed to the package still lying on the foyer floor. She had a sudden sense of foreboding. She must get rid of the package — before her aunt and cousin came downstairs.

The burlap wrapping was ice cold. Had it been cold before? Shivering, Minabell managed to get her paws hooked through the rough twine. She pulled the parcel into the hallway and hurriedly looked around. All the rooms on the ground floor opened onto the great hall. Where could she hide it?

The music room was the closest, the first door on the right. She dragged the parcel across the polished oak floor and through the doorway. Aunt Pitty Pat's gold harp stood in the middle of the room, and delicate gilt chairs were arranged in a semicircle around the harp. There didn't seem to be any hiding place.

She looked at the hearth. Every room in the manor had its own fireplace, built of prairie pebbles. And most of them had a few stones loose at floor level. Each time she scrubbed or swept the floor, these stones were pushed out and had to be put back.

Huffing and puffing, she pulled the parcel across the room. She found two loose pebbles on the left side of the fireplace. She removed them and shoved the package into the hole. There was just enough room to replace one of the stones. One stone was left.

Aunt Pitty Pat and Cousin Violet Mae were on their way down the stairs. She could hear them on the landing. Minabell ran to the window, lifted it up, and dropped the pebble on the ground.

"Good-evening, Percy," said Aunt Pitty Pat, her voice now coming from the hall. "Minabell, where are you? Percy Bat is here." He must have come in the back way, through the kitchen. She heard her aunt introducing him to Cousin Violet Mae.

A sudden chill left Minabell feeling weak,

and she thought for a moment she was going to faint. She stumbled against a plant stand holding a small wilted flower in a clay pot. It was a dying morning-glory plant her aunt had been trying to nurse back to health. Minabell steadied herself and walked out into the hall.

"There you are. . . ." Aunt Pitty Pat stared at Minabell.

"Little miss," cried Percy, running to her side. "What's wrong?"

Teeth chattering, Minabell collapsed onto a hall bench, feeling as wilted as the flower.

Aunt Pitty Pat hurriedly brought a wool shawl and wrapped it around Minabell's shoulders. "You must be catching the prairie flu, mouseling. Land sakes! Your paws are freezing," she said, rubbing them between her own.

Cousin Violet Mae took a hasty step away from Minabell. She whipped an atomizer from her purse and sprayed her throat. "One can't be too careful with flu germs," she said with a dainty toss of her head.

Minabell knew she wasn't catching the prairie flu. It was the parcel. There was something evil about the burlap-wrapped package. Just touching it had cast a spell over her, draining away her strength and chilling her to the bone.

She slumped on the bench, feeling guilty for not telling her aunt about the package. They never kept secrets from each other. She looked up at Aunt Pitty Pat's troubled face and was tempted to tell her.

As she gazed into her aunt's loving eyes, the uneasy feeling of danger and foreboding returned. No, she decided. She would say nothing until she found out what was inside the parcel. There was no need to worry Aunt Pitty Pat, and perhaps ruin Cousin Violet Mae's visit. Tomorrow she would open the package. But tonight they had guests waiting and supper to serve.

With this decision, she sat up straight and took a deep breath. Her chills and weakness began to disappear. Clear thinking and a sensible plan of action were having their good effect.

"I'm feeling much better," she assured her aunt. And to prove her point, she put aside the shawl and got to her feet. Although still a bit shaky, she squared her shoulders and stood tall. "See, Aunty? I'm fine."

Aunt Pitty Pat was relieved. "Come," she said, leading the way into the dining room. "It's way past dinnertime, and our guests must be hungry."

Percy Bat nodded his head eagerly. After his long winter's hibernation, he was anxiously awaiting his first meal of the new season. Minabell and her aunt always made a great fuss over Percy's coming-out day and served his favorite food.

Dinner was soon ready. The food had been prepared ahead of time and had only to be warmed up. Aunt Pitty Pat had cooked her special grasshopper-wing stew. And Minabell had made extra large acornburgers smothered in fried prairie grass. For dessert

they planned to serve the first wild straw-
berries of the season, topped with thickly
whipped sap from the spring milkweed.

But dinner was suddenly delayed.

They were just sitting down to eat when
there was a loud banging on the front door.
"Land sakes!" exclaimed Aunt Pitty Pat.
"Who can that be at this late hour?"

3.

The Stranger

"I'm coming, I'm coming." Minabell hurried out of the dining room and across the great hall.

She opened the door to a large, handsome bat. He stood blinking at the brightly lit chandelier, its candles flickering in the sudden breeze. Taking out a pair of sunglasses, he settled them on his hairy nose. "Ah," he murmured, stepping into the foyer, "that's better."

"Allow me to introduce myself," he said with a bow and a flourish of his high silk hat. "Count Von Flittermouse — at your service."

The stranger smiled down at Minabell and swirled his leathery wings, like a great cape, around himself. She stepped back with a startled little "Oh!"

Aunt Pitty Pat hurried toward them, charmed by the stranger's courtly manners. She immediately invited him to spend the night. "Mousehaven Manor never turns away travelers passing through Mousedale," she said warmly. "You are most welcome."

Minabell asked the Count if he would like to bring in his luggage. "I have no luggage, my dear little miss. I like to travel light," he added, chuckling softly. He hesitated. "I do have a rather large wooden . . . ah . . . box outside. But I prefer not to bring it in."

They led Count Von Flittermouse into the dining room and introduced him to their guests. "A fellow Southerner!" he exclaimed, bowing low over Violet Mae's paw. He nodded politely to Percy, who was seated at the table, fork in paw, napkin tied around his neck, hungrily eyeing the food.

"Do join us for dinner, Count," urged Aunt Pitty Pat.

"I've already supped, dear lady," the Count said, his voice deep and melodious. "But I'll keep you company."

And with that, he sat down at the table, crossed his legs, and settled his wings over the back of the chair. He pushed his sunglasses up on his forehead and stared down at them from deep-set, hooded eyes. He grinned broadly, revealing large yellow fangs set well forward and overlapping his thin red lips.

Minabell glanced nervously at her aunt. Aunt Pitty Pat sat, delighted by their visitor, hardly touching her food.

The Count watched with amusement as Percy slurped his grasshopper-wing stew and took huge bites out of his acornburger. The giant bat winked at Minabell. "I see someone is just out of hibernation," he said, making a curious gurgling sound deep in his throat. Minabell suddenly realized he was laughing.

Percy said nothing. With his mouth full, he stared up at the larger bat for a long moment. Then, with a sigh and a hiccup, he continued eating.

After supper the Count stood up, stretched his wings, and said he must be leaving. Aunt Pitty Pat again urged him to spend the night in the manor.

"My dear Ms. Pitty Pat," said Count Von Flittermouse, "a thousand heartfelt thanks for your warm welcome. But I am a creature of the night. I sleep during the daylight hours. And always, my dear lady, I carry my bed with me wherever I go. I enjoy the outdoor life. The night air is so refreshing."

The Count turned to Minabell and asked for directions to Springfield, the state capital of Illinois. "I'm interested in camping out at Oak Ridge Cemetery. I've always longed to visit Lincoln's tomb."

They watched the Count move slowly across the park with an odd lurching shuffle. He walked to a long wooden box lying on the grass, lifted it onto his back, and flew off into the night.

"Land sakes, Minabell!" exclaimed Aunt Pitty Pat. "Could that be the bed he spoke of?"

Puzzled, Minabell gazed up at the great bat, now a black shape against the new moon. "Maybe that's where he keeps his luggage."

"HIC!" blurted out Percy. He placed a wingtip over his mouth, stared down at the floor, and sighed.

"Percy, dear, what's troubling you?" asked Minabell. He was an old friend, and she knew when he was worried and out of sorts. He always hiccupped and sighed. And he had been hiccupping and sighing all evening.

Percy avoided her eyes and didn't answer her question. "Good-night," he muttered. "Thank you for my coming-out dinner," he added hastily as he flew out the door and up to his home in the bell tower.

"I think Percy has indigestion," said Aunt

Pitty Pat. "He always gulps his food too fast when he comes out of hibernation."

"How gross!" murmured Cousin Violet Mae.

"Come, dear," said Aunt Pitty Pat, leading her niece up the stairs to her bedroom. "Don't be long, mouseling," she called down to Minabell. "You need your sleep, too."

Minabell went back to the dining room to collect the dishes. She noticed something odd. A fine, gray, powdery dust covered the back and seat of the chair where the Count had been sitting. On checking closer, it looked like dandruff. Well, she decided, whatever it is, I'll clean it up tomorrow.

Minabell carried the supper dishes along the hall to the old-fashioned kitchen and stacked them in the sink. They would wash them in the morning.

Locking the doors, she turned out the lights and climbed the stairs to her bedroom. She paused a moment on the landing and looked down. Was there a hint of movement — a shadow flying past the fan window above the front door? She waited. It didn't appear again.

She yawned . . . just her imagination. This had been a tiring day. Aunt Pitty Pat was right. It was time for bed.

4.

Who's There?

Minabell started up in bed, her heart pounding. Moonlight flooded in through the bedroom window, tightly closed against the chill spring air. The ticking of the clock on the dresser was the only sound in the room. And yet . . .

What had awakened her?

She glanced nervously about. The furniture looked large and menacing in the dark. She shook her head and twitched her sidewhiskers. You're imagining things, she told herself. Stop acting like a baby mouseling.

Minabell lay down again and pulled up the blanket. She was just drifting off when she heard someone shuffling along the balcony outside her door. "Aunt Pitty Pat?" she called. There was no answer. The shuffling sound stopped.

Minabell slipped out of bed, tiptoed to the door, and peered out. She looked up and down the hallway, but saw no one.

The grand staircase arose from the great hall on the first floor and ended on the balcony. All the bedrooms opened onto the balcony. She stood a moment, listening. Was there the faintest whisper of sound in the stairwell — the soft flapping of retreating wings? She looked over the banister. It was dark and silent in the hall below.

Minabell could dimly make out the chandelier hanging from its chain into the shadows. The chandelier was swaying, causing the crystal prisms to tinkle softly. There must be a slight breeze, she thought. But that couldn't be — all the windows were closed and locked.

Minabell shivered. It would be nice, she

thought, to forget the last few minutes and snuggle into bed with her aunt.

She ran silently along the gallery to her aunt's bedroom and peeked in. Aunt Pitty Pat was fast asleep, and Minabell decided not to disturb her.

Minabell ran back to her own room and climbed into bed. But sleep wouldn't come. Her mind wandered to the Prairie Pirates, and their leader, Magnus Rat. The trouble had happened over a year ago, but it was still fresh in her memory. The Pirates had captured Mousehaven Manor and imprisoned her aunt. With the help of Secret Agent Wendell Weasel and her friends from Rodentville, Minabell had saved her aunt and recaptured the manor.

After that, Aunt Pitty Pat had put Minabell in charge of security. She wore the master keys to Mousehaven Manor on her belt. They jingled comfortingly at her waist during the day and were laid aside only at night.

Minabell jumped out of bed and ran to

her dresser. The belt was where she had left it, and all the keys were on the keyring. She remembered bolting and locking the doors before coming upstairs.

Minabell went back to bed and fell into a deep, uneasy sleep as moonlight crept across her blanket.

5.

Rhinestone Rodent

The moment Minabell awoke she remembered — the window! She ran downstairs. "Tail feathers!" she muttered. The music room door was wide open, and a brisk wind was blowing into the hall. She had forgotten to close and lock the window after throwing out the pebble the night before. She looked up. The chandelier was still swaying and tinkling.

So it hadn't been her imagination. Some creature had slipped through the music room window last night and crept about the manor. She was certain she had heard someone shuffling past her bedroom. Was it a thief? She searched the downstairs rooms. There wasn't anything missing.

Minabell ran upstairs and aroused her aunt. Together they checked out the balcony rooms. Nothing had been disturbed.

"Let's not tell Violet Mae," said Aunt Pitty Pat. "We don't want to alarm her." She gave Minabell's paw a comforting pat. "Perhaps you imagined it, mouseling," she added as she bustled off to prepare breakfast.

Minabell knew better. She wandered into the music room and sat down on a gilt chair. It was her fault. I've been careless, she thought, touching the keyring on her belt.

Since nothing had been stolen, perhaps someone was searching for something and hadn't found it. But what? The package! She ran to the fireplace and peeked behind the stone. The parcel was still there.

Sighing with worry, she closed and locked the window. "Like closing the barn door after the cat is out," she whispered.

The room was still cold. The chill was

coming from the package, of course. But it would have to wait. There was no time to examine it now. There was shopping to be done.

❧

Minabell stepped out of the bakery and strolled down Mousedale's Main Street with her basket full of hot-cross buns. She nodded pleasantly to friends doing their daily shopping and stopped now and then to gaze into store windows.

Springtime on the Illinois prairie, her favorite time of year. She took a deep breath of the rainwashed air, determined to forget her worries and enjoy herself.

A sign in front of the Mousedale Music Hall caught her eye.

Now Appearing in Concert

* * *

RHINESTONE RODENT

* * *

Featuring the Velvet Voice
of the Singing Mouse from Texas
and His Magic Rope Tricks

Minabell crossed the street to the music hall and, on a sudden impulse, bought a ticket to the matinee. The show had already started, but she found a seat in the back of the darkened theater. "Praise the prairie skies," she whispered, staring up at the handsome mouse singing on stage.

He was dressed all in black, but he sparkled like Aunt Pitty Pat's chandelier. His Western hat, vest, and boots were encrusted with brilliant stones. Every inch of his costume was covered with rhinestones that glittered in the spotlight.

Rhinestone Rodent finished his song and set aside his guitar. He removed the two coiled ropes from his belt and stood quietly, looking out over the audience. "YIPPEEE!"

He leapt into the air, twirling one of the ropes high overhead. He landed gracefully, and with a quick twist of his paw, sent the other rope whirling in a wide circle at his side. He jumped in and out of this second lariat to the cheers and whistles of the audience.

After several curtain calls and shouts of *"Encore! Encore!"* he came back onstage and picked up his guitar. Moving to center stage, he began crooning a familiar old ballad.

> "Under Texas skies
> Where white clouds
> Billow.
> I buried my mousie
> Under a weeping
> Willow.
> Farewell, farewell!

> "Oh, tiny, whiskery
> Texas nose.
> Oh, sharp and tiny
> Texas toes.
> Farewell, farewell!"

Minabell wiped away a tear. And in the hushed silence, sniffles could be heard from the audience.

"Bravo! Bravo!" The audience was on their feet, loudly clapping, giving Rhinestone

Rodent a standing ovation.

The show was over. Minabell stepped out of the music hall and stood blinking in the afternoon sunlight. She had been gone too long. Aunt Pitty Pat and Cousin Violet Mae would be waiting to have tea. The hot-cross buns were her aunt's teatime favorites.

A sudden shout, followed by frightened cries, came from the end of Main Street. Mousewives and their little ones ran past her. Shopkeepers stepped out of the stores with puzzled looks on their faces. Windows were slammed open, and small creatures leaned out, straining to see up the street.

Minabell lifted her pink nose and tested the air. "Oh, no!" she whispered.

6.

Danger!

"Fire!" shouted someone, and the cry was taken up by others. "Fire! Fire! The manor is on fire!"

Minabell dropped her basket, and the hot-cross buns tumbled out and rolled into the gutter. But she didn't notice. "Aunt Pitty Pat!" she cried as she ran down the street, pushing her way through the crowd.

All the streets of the village opened onto the parkway surrounding Mousehaven Manor. Minabell came to the end of the street and stared out across the park. The manor was, indeed, on fire.

The ancient mansion, built of multicolored

prairie pebbles, shimmered in the May sun. But behind the first-floor windows Minabell saw leaping flames, and smoke poured out of the half-open front door.

With a sudden loud *WHOOSH*, and a shattering of glass, the music room windows blew out. Orange flames shot out into the afternoon sunlight.

"Ohhhhh!" moaned the crowd.

The great bell in the tower began to ring. Minabell looked up. Percy Bat, of course. He was doing his duty, ringing the bell, sending a message of danger out over the countryside.

After the trouble with the Prairie Pirates, Percy had been put in charge of the bell. He and his large family lived in the tower, and they could always be counted on in an emergency.

The sound of the bell alerted the crowd. Every able-bodied creature in the village joined forces, and a water brigade was organized. They formed a long line from the village pond to the manor. Buckets of water were sent flying from paw to paw and the water thrown on the flames.

Minabell joined the line and helped pass the splashing pails along. Trembling with fright, she tried not to glance at the flaming mansion. She kept her attention on the task at hand.

The bell stopped tolling, and Minabell quickly handed the last bucket to the next one in line. Then she rushed toward the manor, calling her aunt's name. A moment later Aunt Pitty Pat came running from around the side of the manor, followed by Percy.

"Mouseling!" cried Aunt Pitty Pat. "You're safe! But where . . . ? Oh, dearie me! Your cousin . . . have you seen Violet Mae?"

"I thought she was with you."

"No," said Aunt Pitty Pat. "I was setting the table for tea in the back parlor. I smelled smoke and ran out into the hall to investigate. But I didn't see Violet Mae."

"She wasn't with me," said Percy, shielding his watering eyes with a wingtip. He always had trouble seeing in the sunlight. "I was in the bell chamber ringing the tower bell."

Minabell looked around, searching the crowd for her cousin. The fire had finally been put out, and the tired water brigade was straggling back to the village. There had been a great amount of smoke and fire, but it had been contained in the entrance hall and the music room.

Rhinestone Rodent left a group of admirers and hurried toward them. "My, oh, my!" whispered Aunt Pitty Pat, staring at the handsome creature.

Politely removing his Western hat, Rhinestone introduced himself. Then he addressed Minabell in a friendly Texas drawl. "Howdy, ma'am. Can I be of help? Is everyone here?"

"Oh, no!" cried Minabell, suddenly remembering. "Cousin Violet Mae is missing! She must still be inside."

They all turned and ran for the manor door. Percy Bat, slower than the others, crowded in behind them, grateful to be out of the sun.

Aunt Pitty Pat stared at the mess in the hall. Her beautifully polished oak floors were awash in pond water, and the walls were streaked with smoke.

"Cousin Violet Mae," shouted Minabell. "Are you here?"

There was no answer. Minabell called again.

"Fiddle dee dee, Cousin Minabell. What's all the fuss about?" The sweet soprano voice came floating down from above, and so did Miss Violet Mae Mouse.

She slowly walked down the grand staircase, lightly trailing a paw along the banister. Her lavender beaded purse swung by a silken cord from the other paw.

"Oh, thank the prairie skies!" sighed Aunt Pitty Pat. "You're safe."

Violet Mae stopped midway down the stairs and removed her paw from the banister. She wrinkled her small pink nose in distaste. Then she took a lace-edged handkerchief from her purse and wiped the smoke soot from her paw. She dropped the soiled kerchief on the stair. "I do declare, Aunt Pitty Pat," she said with a pout, "the housekeeping at Mousehaven Manor is not up to our Southern standards."

Aunt Pitty Pat took a deep breath and did not reply.

Minabell put an arm around her aunt and gave her a sympathetic squeeze. "Cousin Violet Mae," she said patiently, "where have you been? The manor was on fire, and we couldn't find you. We were worried."

"Why, Cousin Minabell, honey, I know nothing about a fire. I've been upstairs in my room, taking a nap. I do need my beauty rest."

Violet Mae suddenly noticed Rhinestone Rodent standing in the doorway, his costume flashing in the sunlight. "Cousin Minabell," she said, her voice sharp, "where do you keep your manners?" She stared down at the sparkling rodent. "We have not been properly introduced, sir."

Rhinestone stepped forward, and Minabell made the introductions. Violet Mae opened her purse and removed a black lace fan. Holding it in front of her face, she fluttered her long eyelashes at Rhinestone. "Charmed, I'm sure," she said.

There was a sudden creaking and groaning from above, and they stared up at the ceiling. The chandelier was swaying on its chain. As they watched, the screw holding the chain slowly pulled free from the water-soaked beam.

They jumped aside just as the chandelier came crashing down with a great splashing of pond water and the jingle-jangle of breaking prisms.

"Oh, mouseling!" cried Aunt Pitty Pat.

7.

Rhinestone's Secret

Minabell hired workmice from the village to make repairs and clean up the worst of the damage. They washed and painted the smoke-stained walls and replaced the glass in the music room windows.

The harp had lost its strings in the fire. Minabell and her aunt decided it could be mended. But nothing could replace Aunt Pitty Pat's beautiful chandelier. It had been completely destroyed. Only the metal frame remained. Minabell had it hauled down to the manor's dungeon.

Aunt Pitty Pat tried to remain cheerful. "Thank the prairie stars nobody was hurt," she said with a slight quaver in her voice.

"We were very lucky," agreed Minabell gently.

"Cousin Minabell — Aunt Pitty Pat!" Violet Mae stood pouting in the parlor doorway, paws on hips. "I've been looking everywhere for you. Have you forgotten my tea party? My guest will be here any moment."

"Oh, dearie me," cried Aunt Pitty Pat, hurrying out of the room and down the hall to the kitchen. A moment later she appeared, carrying a tray heaped with candied black-eyed Susans. "It was all prepared, dear." Puffing a bit, she set the tray on the table and helped Minabell set out the tea service.

"Fiddle dee dee!" cried Cousin Violet Mae. "Just look at this room. It's *so* old-fashioned. Whatever will Mr. Rodent think of us?"

She had invited Rhinestone to be her guest at tea and insisted that it be a grand occasion. Ever since their chance meeting on the stairway a week ago, they had seen much of each other. Indeed, Rhinestone had lost his heart to the pretty little Southerner. For her part, Violet Mae was thrilled to be seen in the company of the handsome matinee idol in his jewel-studded costume.

Violet Mae glanced at the parlor table. The preparations for tea were coming along nicely. While Cousin Minabell set the table with their best china, Violet Mae removed a small can of talcum from her purse. She sprinkled herself generously with the powder. A lilac-scented cloud drifted toward the ceiling.

Humming a pretty tune, she plumped up the pillows and sat down on the couch with a box of bonbons, a gift from Rhinestone. She took her time selecting a chocolate and, with a happy little sigh, nibbled daintily.

"You'll spoil your appetite, dear," said Aunt Pitty Pat, coming in with a plate full of cucumber sandwiches.

There was a knock at the front door.

"I do declare, who could that be?" sang out Cousin Violet Mae, starting up and running from the room.

"Ehhhhhhhhhh!" came a shriek from the foyer. Minabell and her aunt rushed into the hall. Violet Mae was leaning against the wall, her eyes squeezed shut.

A stranger, dressed in black, stood in the doorway. It was Rhinestone Rodent, but they hardly recognized him. All the jewels had been removed from his costume. From the top of his Western hat to the bottom of his Western boots not a rhinestone sparkled or caught the afternoon sunlight.

"My smelling salts," cried Cousin Violet Mae, fumbling with her purse. Aunt Pitty Pat ran to help her.

Rhinestone beckoned Minabell into the foyer and removed a leather pouch from inside his vest. Without a word, he opened it and handed it to her. The bag was filled with rhinestones.

"What . . .?"

"Shhhhh!" said Rhinestone. "I took them from my costume."

Minabell stared at his vest, hat, and boots. There were torn threads and small holes where he had ripped them off.

"This is a surprise for Aunt Pitty Pat," he murmured. "It'll be our secret." He leaned close and whispered his plans in her ear. "Do you think we can manage it?"

Minabell's eyes shone. "Oh, my, yes!" she said. "I'll ask Percy to help us."

"It's my way of saying thank you," said Rhinestone. "If it hadn't been for you and Aunt Pitty Pat, I might never have met my sweet Violet Mae."

Cousin Violet Mae hid behind her fan and sulked. She refused to look at the new, plain Rhinestone. Finally, he told her of the costume being made for him by Mousedale's finest seamstress. "I designed it myself," he assured her. "It'll be the most beautiful outfit north of the Texas Panhandle."

All was forgiven. After a pleasant tea, they strolled arm in arm across the parkway. Cousin Violet Mae swung her beaded purse, twirled her lavender parasol, and fluttered her long lashes as she gazed up at Rhinestone.

Minabell and her aunt watched them from the parlor window. "They make a handsome couple," said Aunt Pitty Pat. She had high hopes for a wedding at Mousehaven Manor in the very near future. "Perhaps we'll have a June bride," she whispered, side-whiskers quivering at the thought.

Minabell was to remember Aunt Pitty Pat's hopeful words in the troublesome days that followed.

8.

The Magic Water

Minabell and Percy walked about the music room, searching for clues to how the fire was started. The two friends were alone in the manor. Aunt Pitty Pat and Cousin Violet Mae had just left for the Mousedale Music Hall. Rhinestone Rodent had invited them to be his guests at the matinee.

Minabell noticed a trail of gray dust — footprints on the floor. It was the same kind of dust she had found in the dining room. She remembered seeing it on the chair where Count Von Flittermouse had been sitting.

Percy examined the charred remains of

two gilt chairs. "Look at these, Minabell. They were broken up and used as kindling to start the fire."

"Who would want to burn down the manor?" Minabell asked.

"Whoever it was didn't want to destroy the manor. A small fire was set to draw our attention — distract us so someone could ransack the house. Is anything missing?"

Minabell turned and stared at the fireplace. "There is something . . . but . . . it's not missing. I checked."

Percy followed her gaze. "What is it, little miss?"

Minabell studied her friend's gentle face, his brow wrinkled with concern. She decided to tell him about the package. She blurted it out before she could change her mind.

"The prairie hawk left it here, Percy. There was no name or address on the parcel, but he had instructions to give it to no one but me."

"What's in the package?"

"I don't know." They ran to the fireplace. "It's in here," Minabell said, pushing aside the pebble.

They pulled the package out of the crevice and into the light. Percy watched Minabell loosen the string and peel back the rotting burlap. A piece of paper fell out of one of the folds.

"Oh!" Minabell stared down at the paper. It had her name handwritten under the official seal of the ISSP — Illinois State Ski Patrol. She snatched it up and opened it. "Oh, dear!" she exclaimed again.

Percy hiccupped twice and sighed.

"Sorry, Percy," murmured Minabell and read the note out loud.

Minabell,
    I'm sending you this ancient box for safekeeping. Guard it well. There are forces of evil abroad on the prairie who will try to steal it. The document inside the box will explain everything.
    This treasure was held by Violet Mae's family for over four hundred years. It was a well-kept

secret handed down to the head of the Mouse
family from one generation to the next.

Each caretaker is honor-bound not to use the
contents of the box for personal gain. It must only
be used for the good of all.

Violet Mae knows nothing about it. Her
guardian, Colonel Mouse, of St. Augustine,
Florida, was the last caretaker of the box. On his
deathbed he asked that the box (and Violet Mae)
be delivered into your care.

I know you are equal to the task.
Your friend,

Wendell Weasel

Secret Agent Wendell Weasel
Illinois State Ski Patrol

Minabell folded the letter and placed it
in her pouch. "This is official state business,"
she said. "I will help in any way I can."

She removed the rest of the burlap wrapping and uncovered a small mahogany box
with the initials *J.D.R.* carved on the top.
The lid was hinged with strips of leather on
one side, and held closed on the other with
a tarnished silver clasp.

As they watched, something trickled out from under the lid, ran down the side of the box, and formed a small heap on the floor.

"Looks like sand," Percy said. "White sand."

Minabell pulled up the silver clasp and opened the box. Percy was right. It was filled to the top with pure white sand. Sticking out of the center was a cork stopper. She reached out and touched it.

"Whiskers and tail feathers!" she muttered, blowing on her paw. "It's so cold, it almost feels hot."

"Look at this." Percy removed a folded parchment wedged inside the box's lid. "It must be the document Secret Agent Weasel mentioned," he said, handing it to Minabell. The paper was brown with age, and crackled when she opened it.

"It's a map," she said. "There's writing on the bottom, but I can't read it."

"I think it's written in Spanish," Percy said. "Notice the name signed at the end — Juan de Ratón. Wasn't he a famous Spanish

mouse, the companion of the explorer Ponce de León?"

"Oh, yes," Minabell agreed. "I remember, now — from my history class. They were the ones who discovered Florida."

"Oh, I say! Hic! Oh, dear!"

"What is it, Percy?"

"Weren't they also searching for . . ." Percy hesitated. "The Fountain of Youth!" he added slowly. "It was said the water from the fountain was magic. Anyone who drank it would live forever."

Minabell held her breath and slowly pulled the cork out of the sand. Attached to the cork was a glass vial. A cold white vapor curled around the tiny flask.

"What's inside?"

Minabell held it up to the window. Golden liquid bubbled and swirled in the vial.

9.

Bats in the Belfry

Minabell opened the door under the grand staircase and turned on her flashlight. She ran down the narrow flight of steps and entered Mousehaven Manor's root cellar, famous throughout Sangamon County.

This was one of her favorite places in the manor. Her mouth watered at the aroma of delicious food — dried fruits and vegetables — piled up high in the bins lining the walls. Above the bins, sturdy shelves held row upon row of Aunt Pitty Pat's jams and jellies.

But she mustn't linger. Percy was waiting. This afternoon they were going to Indian

Mound Hill to consult Madame Froganna, the fortune-teller, about the Spanish map. Ducking under the drying herbs hanging from the rafters, she went down another flight of stairs and stood in front of the manor's dungeon. Removing a key from the keyring on her belt, she unlocked the oaken door and swung it open.

Minabell had once been held captive in this dungeon, and she never entered without a slight shiver of memory. She shined the flashlight over the walls. Water dripped down and puddled on the cobblestones. In the corner lay the broken chandelier, the metal frame resting on the wet floor.

She quickly crossed the room and slipped through a door held open by a large stone. This was the entrance to a secret passageway that led up to the bell tower. Only three creatures in the state knew of this secret entrance — she, Aunt Pitty Pat, and Percy. Tucking the flashlight into her belt, Minabell ran to the end of the corridor and climbed the wooden ladder built into the wall.

She crawled through the trapdoor in the ceiling and climbed out into another corridor. Directly ahead was a winding stairway, dimly lit by a slit window on the first landing. Minabell had made this trip often. It was the only way to get up to Percy's quarters — unless one could fly.

Minabell turned off her flashlight and checked her belt-pouch. The folded map was safely tucked inside. Hurrying up the stairs, she stepped out into Percy's domain — the bell tower — and stood blinking in the afternoon sun.

The tower, open to the sky on three sides, had been the Bat family's home for many years. Hanging from the center of the turret was the great bell. A heavy rope ran down to a hole in the floorboards. The rope went through this opening to a small room next to the manor's front door. This was the room where Percy rang the bell in time of trouble, sending an alarm ringing out over the prairie.

Above the bell lived 110 small, brown bats, clinging upside down from the rafters.

They were Percy's relatives — his mother and father, brothers and sisters, aunts and uncles, cousins by the dozens, and grandmas and grandpas. A shy group, they spent their days sleeping and their nights out on the prairie, feeding on insects. In the late afternoon they loved to gossip, contentedly squeaking bat secrets to each other as they watched the sun set behind the manor.

The bats are unusually quiet this afternoon, Minabell thought, glancing up. Two hundred and twenty wary eyes stared back. But they were not staring at her. She followed their gaze.

On the farther side of the tower, on the parapet surrounding the belfry, stood Count Von Flittermouse. He was deep in conversation with Percy, whose back was to Minabell. "No!" Percy was saying, "I know nothing about a package."

The Count, who was facing Minabell, suddenly noticed her in the doorway. "Ah, Ms. Mouse," he said smoothly, removing his high hat. He stared at the arched entryway. "A secret entrance, Ms. Mouse? How delightfully mysterious."

He fluttered down from the parapet. The bats in the rafters let out a squeal of alarm as all eyes turned, following the Count's movements.

He landed with a *thunk* directly in front of Minabell, and a cloud of dust rose up from the patchy fur on his body. "Whiskers and tail feathers!" she whispered. In the light of day she could see the Count dyed his fur brown. A mouse-inch of gray showed at the roots all over his body.

Sunlight, filtering through his wings, revealed a network of veins and wrinkles covering the leathery surface. How very old he is, she thought.

The Count removed his sunglasses and gazed down at her with bloodshot, watery eyes. "I am checking on a package I've — er — mislaid. I thought it might have been sent to Mousehaven Manor by mistake, Ms. Mouse."

Percy, who had turned quickly to face

her, gave a slight shake of his head.

Minabell swallowed hard and shook her head, too. The Count was standing too close. She tried to lean back — away from him. But he moved closer, pinning her to the doorframe with his great belly. A musty smell of moth-eaten fur gagged her.

"No," she managed to squeak, "nothing has been delivered to the manor." She gave a nervous little giggle and tried a feeble joke. "Nothing except Cousin Violet Mae, of course."

The Count laughed politely. So did Percy and the bats in the rafters. The belfry was suddenly awash in forced merriment.

In the silence that followed, the Count stared gravely at Minabell.

Percy hiccupped.

The Count spoke softly. "This is not a joking matter, Ms. Mouse. It is of the utmost importance that I find this package — immediately. Time is running out," he added, as if speaking to himself.

He stepped back from Minabell, and she sighed with relief. "The package I'm looking for, Ms. Mouse, is quite a bit smaller than the person of Ms. Violet Mae."

Minabell's paw crept to her belt-pouch and the reassuring feel of the map. Too late — she realized what she had done and snatched her paw away.

The Count's eyes darted to the pouch. He made a sudden grab for it. Minabell jumped to the side, just as Percy dived down from the parapet and spread his wings in front of her.

There came a soft hissing from above. The Count lifted his head on his scrawny neck and stared up at the rafters.

Two hundred and twenty small, round eyes stared back at him. One hundred and ten pairs of lips curled back in silent snarls. Two hundred and twenty needle-sharp fangs glistened in the rafters' shadows.

Count Von Flittermouse was outnumbered. Saying not a word, he put on his sunglasses and jumped into the air. With a flurry of wings, he flew out of the bell tower. Behind him a cloud of gray dandruff, skin-scales, and dyed fur settled slowly to the floorboards.

10.

Cross My Paw with Silver

Daylight was fading as Minabell climbed aboard Percy's back, seated herself comfortably, and took a firm grip on his neck-fur. With a hasty good-bye to his relatives, Percy flew from the tower.

Spread out below them was a bat's-eye view of the Illinois prairie and the village of Mousedale. The evening star winked on just as they arrived at Indian Mound Hill. They floated gently down and settled at the entrance of Madame Froganna's well-lit cave.

Madame Froganna herself was enjoying the evening breeze. Lazily blinking her eyes, she squatted in her doorway, looking like a large, green, overripe apple. A red turban sat on her head, and a fringed shawl covered her plump shoulders.

She grinned down at them. "Cross my paw with silver," she cried, enfolding Minabell in a hearty embrace. "Good-evening, Percy." The bangles and beads around her neck jingled merrily as she led them into her home.

She waved her apron at her children leapfrogging about the cave. "Out, out!" she shouted good-naturedly. They paid no attention to their mother but continued to chase each other about the room.

In one corner, a kettle of soup bubbled over a fire. A table and four chairs stood in the center of the room. Madame made a swipe at the seats of the chairs with her apron and invited Minabell and Percy to take a load off.

Madame Froganna lowered herself onto a chair and studied her guests with a knowing eye. "Trouble?" she asked. Minabell was about to answer when one of Madame's children made a flying leap and landed on top of her mother's turban.

"This is my eldest daughter, Frogella," said Madame. "You can speak freely. She's learning the family business."

Minabell hesitated. But Frogella was clearly staying. She grinned happily, a miniature copy of her mother. Settling herself into a comfortable position, she stared expectantly down at Minabell. "Cross my paw with silver," she lisped.

Minabell took two silver pebbles from her pouch. She gave one to Madame and handed the other up to Frogella. Then she brought out the map and spread it on the table.

"We can't read it," Percy said.

Madame squinted at the map. "I'm not surprised. It's in Spanish. Look at this." She pointed to a date in faded brown ink. "This was written in 1513. Why — this is over four hundred years old."

"Can you read it?" asked Minabell.

"Do toads have warts?" asked Madame,

putting on her glasses. "I used to live south of the border — down Mexico way." She studied the writing below the map and began translating.

Be it known that I and my good companion and shipmate, Captain Ponce de Le̦ón, have on this day discovered a spring of fresh, sweet water on the fair land we have named Florida. The Indians of these parts claim the water gives life everlasting. We have named the spring — Fountain of Youth.
Recorded on this fifth day of April, in the year 1513.
Signed:

Seamouse, First Class
Juan de Ratón

"What's this?" Minabell pointed to a spot on the map marked with an X. Madame read the faded scrawl underneath.

X marks the spot wherein lies the Fountain of Youth. Sample of the Magic Water taken from the spring by Seamouse J. de R.

65

"Thundering toadstools!!" cried Madame. "I've heard of this Magic Water. It's said that anyone who drinks it will live for hundreds of years."

"We have the sample of the Magic Water," Minabell said.

"Hush!" yelled Madame. "The walls have ears."

Frogella poked her head out from under a fold of the turban. "Large bat in a high hat," she whispered.

"Quite right, my dear," approved Madame. "Thank you for reminding me." She flicked out her tongue, catching one of her children who was about to fall into the soup. She tossed him back in the corner with his brothers and sisters.

"There was a large brown bat here yesterday," Madame continued. "He was nosing around the Hill, asking questions about a parcel he had lost."

"Count Von Flittermouse!" Percy said.

Speaking softly, Minabell told them of the package delivered to her by the prairie hawk, and of the letter from Secret Agent Wendell Weasel giving the package into her care.

"I hope you have it hidden in a safe place," said Madame, stifling a yawn. It was catching. Soon they were all yawning.

"Time to go," said Minabell. "Aunt Pitty Pat will be worried."

"Good-night," said Frogella, jumping off the turban. She joined her brothers and sisters, piled on top of each other, fast asleep in the cave's shadows.

Minabell folded the map and put it back in her pouch. She and Percy thanked Madame Froganna and slipped out of the warm cave. Madame bolted the door behind them.

They stood shivering under the crescent moon, listening to the wind sigh through the branches of the elm tree.

11.

The Shape-Changer

The murmur of the wind in the elm tree was drowned out by an unearthly wail.

Minabell drew close to Percy. "What is *that*?" she whispered.

Percy faced into the wind. The sound seemed to be coming from that direction. But abruptly the fearsome cry surrounded them. It came from all sides at once. At that moment the moon disappeared, and the evening star winked out. The prairie wind stopped blowing.

Percy used his sonar to search the darkness. He sensed nothing. Minabell fumbled for the flashlight at her waist and turned it on.

The beam of her light was directed down at the ground a few mousefeet away. In its bright circle they saw two hairy paws with long claws hugging the ground. Trembling, she slowly moved the beam upward.

A huge prairie wolf sat on its haunches directly in their path. His eyes glowed red, and silvery drool hung from his thin lips.

"Surprise, surprise, Ms. Minabell Mouse," said the wolf. "We meet by flashlight," he added gaily.

Minabell stood her ground. "How do you know my name, sir? I don't believe we've met."

Percy let out a startled squeak. "Oh, no!" he whispered.

The creature gave a wide, sharp-fanged grin. "Oh, yes, my dear Percival." He reached into the shadows, produced a high hat, and slapped it on his head. "The one and only — Count Von Flittermouse," he said with a bow.

"It was you . . . hic . . . you started the fire in the manor."

"Correct, again, my dear fellow. I didn't find the vial then, but — I have now." The prairie wolf grinned down at Minabell.

"What — how — ?" Minabell recognized the Count's voice and his hat — but she didn't understand.

"Shape-changing," cried the Count. "One of the many talents of my kind."

"What kind is that?" asked Minabell.

"Tell her, Percival."

Percy hiccupped and sighed. "I'm afraid he's a *vampire* bat, Minabell. I've known it since the first night he came to the manor, but I was too ashamed to tell you. He's a disgrace to the entire Bat family."

"Sticks and stones, Percy!" The prairie wolf threw back his head and let out a joyous howl.

As the wolf's cry died away, the wind started up, rattling the branches of the nearby trees.

From the valley came the pealing of Mousehaven Manor's great bell. Loud and clear — "Danger! — danger! — danger!"

The wolf cocked his head, listening. He gnashed his teeth and glared at Minabell. "Give it to me."

"Give you what, sir?"

"The vial. I know you have it." He lurched forward and tore the pouch off her belt.

With a cry, Minabell tried to grab it back.

The vampire slapped the pouch down between his paws. "Here it is, Ms. Minabell. Come and get it." He snapped at the air in front of her nose.

The bell continued to toll.

Three things happened all at once. The moon slipped out from behind the cloud. The evening star winked on again. And they heard singing.

"Under Texas skies
Where white clouds
Billow.
I buried my mousie
Under a weeping
Willow.
Farewell, farewell!"

Rhinestone Rodent appeared over a rise and stopped. He stared at the wolf. "Er . . . howdy, pardner . . . ah . . . er . . . lovely evening for a stroll."

"Look out, Rhinestone!" shouted Minabell. "Run!"

With a growl, the beast turned toward the Texas mouse.

Minabell rushed forward to get her pouch. But the wolf whirled around and grabbed her by the tail.

Rhinestone took in the scene at a glance. He stepped back and quickly removed the lassos from his belt. "YIPPEE!" he yelled, throwing one of them at the wolf's hind leg. "Contact," he cried as the rope found its target. He jumped back, looped it about the tree trunk, and tied a scout's half-hitch knot.

The wolf let go of Minabell and spun about, biting angrily at the rope.

Minabell snatched up her pouch and ran to help Rhinestone.

Rhinestone threw his second lasso and caught the creature's front leg. Minabell seized the other end from Rhinestone and ran to Percy. Silently she pointed up to the top of the elm tree.

Percy clutched the rope to his chest and flew up to the topmost limb. He wrapped it around and around the branch. With a cry of surprise the wolf was hoisted up in the air, stretched between heaven and earth.

The prairie wolf abruptly fell silent and stopped straining against the ropes. He shivered, and as they watched, his body changed its shape. He shrank in upon himself and his color turned from gray to brown. Suddenly, in place of the wolf appeared a bat, one fourth the size. It was Count Von Flittermouse. His front paws and back legs, now smaller, easily slipped the bonds of the ropes. He flashed down, scooped up his high hat from the grass and, with a shriek of rage, flew off into the dark.

12.

The Invalid

Sunlight and soft breezes flooded in through the bedroom window. Moans and loud groans came from across the room as Minabell stirred in bed and awoke. Her whole body ached. Even my tail hurts, she thought — especially my tail. She sat up in bed and threw aside the blanket.

"Oh, dear!" she wailed, just as Aunt Pitty Pat came into the room.

"Glory be!" cried her aunt. Minabell's tail was swollen to almost twice its size. Where the prairie wolf had grabbed it the fur was missing, and in its place was a large, angry bruise beginning to turn purple.

Without a word or a question, her aunt set about tenderly examining it. "Praise the prairie skies it's not broken," she said. "But I'm going to apply a skunk-weed dressing to reduce the swelling." After the dressing had been rubbed on, and the tail bandaged to Aunt Pitty Pat's satisfaction, she brought Minabell a cup of hot sweet-clover tea. Only then did she ask what had happened.

Minabell told her about the mysterious package containing the vial of Magic Water, about the shape-changer, Count Von Flittermouse, who was actually a vampire bat, and how he had attacked them the night before on Indian Mound Hill.

"Percy says we must stay inside after the sun goes down, Aunt Pitty Pat. And keep the manor locked tight." Minabell leaned close and whispered, "Percy says the Count comes into his vampire powers only after dark. That's when he becomes a shape-changer."

"Bed rest," interrupted her aunt firmly. "That's what you need, mouseling. A day in bed." She placed a paw on Minabell's forehead. "You don't have a fever. Perhaps you've had a nightmare."

"Please listen, Aunt Pitty Pat," pleaded Minabell. "The Count is after the Magic Water. He's dangerous and . . ."

"Lie down, mouseling." Aunt Pitty Pat glanced at Minabell's bandaged tail and shook her head. "And try to be more careful, dear," she said, giving Minabell's paw a reassuring pat.

Minabell watched her sensible little aunt leave the room.

She doesn't believe me, Minabell worried. And who could blame her?

Minabell was sure the Count would be back searching for the vial. She shuddered, remembering how old and sick he had appeared in the bell tower. She was certain he needed the Magic Water to stay alive.

Minabell was thankful she hadn't told her aunt where the box was hidden. The less Aunt Pitty Pat knew, the safer she would be. Minabell decided she must get the vial out of the manor before nightfall. Even though she always locked the house at night, she sensed they were all in danger as long as the vial was hidden in the music room.

"Here you are," said Aunt Pitty Pat, coming in with her breakfast tray. She set it on the bed and plumped up the pillows. "Now stay in bed, mouseling," she urged as she hurried away.

Minabell nodded her head and said nothing. She didn't want to lie to her aunt. She had no intention of spending the day in bed. She glanced hungrily at the bowl of fried prairie-grass cakes and the glass of milkweed juice. It was her favorite breakfast, but there was no time to eat.

She set the tray of food on her bedside table and looked around the room. She needed something that would allow her to get out of bed, and still give her tail a chance to heal. The basket. It stood next to her bed filled with balls of wool yarn. Aunt Pitty Pat was teaching her to knit. Minabell emptied the basket and stuffed a pillow inside. Then she carefully cradled her bandaged tail on the pillow and tied it down with a length of pink yarn.

She slipped out of bed, placing the basket handle over her shoulder like a sling. She walked across the room with hardly a twinge of pain, and buckled on her keychain belt. Then she stepped out onto the balcony. Holding the basket in place with one paw, she ran down the grand staircase.

If she hurried, she would just catch the mailbird on his morning flight from Mousedale.

13.

Old Friends

Minabell slipped into the music room, removed the glass vial from the mahogany box, and hid it under the pillow in her tail-sling. She hurried outdoors and down the front steps. Gaylord Cardinal, the mailbird, would be flying this way on his return trip to Rodentville.

She looked about. Where was the best place to wait for him? Geronimouse. She ran across the park, stood next to the statue, and faced toward the village.

She didn't have long to wait. Gaylord appeared, flying low over Main Street, the mail-pouch hanging from one wing.

Minabell waved her handkerchief. Gaylord squawked a greeting, banked sharply, and landed on the grass next to the statue. "Good-morning, Minabell. How is your aunt on this fine day? And how are . . . ?" He stared at her bandaged tail. "What happened?"

Minabell told him about Count Von Flittermouse and the terrible night on Indian Mound Hill. She didn't mention the Magic Water.

"Never trust a bat — vampire or any other kind. . . ." declared Gaylord. He glared up at the bell tower. He had never been at ease with Percy and his family.

Minabell hastily changed the subject. She lifted the edge of the pillow in her tail-basket. "Look, Gaylord." The sun touched the cold vial, and vapor rose in the air. She dropped the pillow back in place. "I want you to take this flask to Rodentville and hide it in a safe place."

"Minabell," Gaylord said crossly, "you know I'm not allowed to carry objects that aren't wrapped or stamped. That's against the mailbird's code. Er . . . what is it?"

They were so busy talking they didn't notice a dark shape flying in from the west. A loud flapping of wings announced the newcomer's arrival. Count Von Flittermouse settled on top of Geronimouse's head.

He settled his sunglasses and leered down at Minabell. "My dear Ms. Mouse," he exclaimed, staring at her tail. "An accident? What a pity."

He turned his attention to Gaylord. "Ah, the mailbird — a noble calling, sir."

Gaylord raised his headcrest, accepting the stranger's compliment. He strutted proudly about, puffing out his breast feathers.

The Count smiled at Minabell. "I do believe I'm just in time. Mailing my package out of town? Clever — but not quite clever enough, my dear."

Before Minabell had a chance to give warning, the Count swooped down and grabbed Gaylord's mail-pouch. He shook its contents out on the grass.

Gaylord leapt a foot off the ground, angrily thrashing his wings. "How dare you, sir!" he screeched. "You are defiling the official Illinois mail."

Ignoring Gaylord, the Count pawed through the letters, searching for the box. When he didn't find it, he turned on Minabell. But a small crowd had started to gather, and the Count changed his mind. He jumped into the air, flew across the park, and settled on a cottage rooftop.

The crowd lost interest and drifted away. Minabell helped Gaylord gather up his letters and return them to the pouch.

"Drop the flask in," the mailbird whispered. "I'll take it to Rodentville for you."

Minabell looked across the park. Count Von Flittermouse was sitting on the roof, watching them. She couldn't risk her old friend's life. "I've changed my mind," she whispered back. "Good-bye, Gaylord. Have a safe flight."

14.

Rhinestone's Gift

"**H**oly prairie fire!" muttered Minabell. "That was close." She walked quickly across the park, stumbling in her hurry to get inside the manor. She forced herself not to look back. The Count might be following.

Once safely inside, she locked and bolted the door. Breathless, she leaned against the wall and removed the flask of Magic Water from the basket. She must return it to its hiding place. She hurried across the hall.

"Minabell!" Aunt Pitty Pat was coming down the stairs. "What are you doing out of bed?"

Minabell stopped guiltily, then ducked

into the music room, slipping on the freshly waxed floor. She reached out and grabbed the edge of the plant stand to keep from falling. The vial flew out of her paw! It landed inside the morning-glory pot with such a jolt, the cork stopper popped loose from the neck of the flask. "Oh . . . no!"

Minabell watched helplessly as the liquid drained out. She stared down at a damp spot in the dirt next to the wilted plant. It was all

that remained of the golden water from the Fountain of Youth.

She returned the empty flask to the mahogany box and replaced it in the hearth.

❧

The next day Minabell told Percy about dropping the vial and losing the water.

"I've betrayed my trust to Secret Agent Wendell Weasel," she said. "The agent was counting on me to guard the Magic Water, and now it's lost forever."

"Never mind, little miss," consoled Percy. "At least it's safe from the Count."

Where *was* Count Von Flittermouse? wondered Minabell. He had not been seen for days. Minabell was careful to keep the manor locked and had asked Cousin Violet Mae to stay indoors at night.

"Fiddle dee dee, Cousin Minabell," cried Violet Mae. "My future husband will protect me!" And that was how she announced her engagement to Rhinestone Rodent.

All Mousedale was agog at the news.

Aunt Pitty Pat forgot her aches and pains as she rushed about planning the wedding. She and Cousin Violet Mae spent their days shopping in Mousedale for the happy event. They told no one what they were buying, wanting every detail to be a surprise.

The bridegroom had a surprise of his own. He reminded Minabell of the leather pouch filled with rhinestones he had left with her. "Of course!" said Minabell, running up to her bedroom to get the stones.

Percy agreed to help. He came down from the bell tower to the dungeon, taking the tower stairs and the secret passageway. Minabell unlocked the heavy door, and she and Rhinestone met Percy in this dark chamber where the broken chandelier had been stored.

Together they hauled the metal framework out of the dungeon and into the root cellar. Minabell shoved the door shut behind them, leaving the padlock dangling. "I'll come back later and lock up," she said.

Pushing and pulling, they managed to

drag the frame across the root cellar and up the basement stairs to the great hall.

They emptied the pouch and strung the rhinestones on the frame where the broken prisms had been before. Then they reset the rows of candles. When it was finished and the chain attached, Minabell and Rhinestone held up the new chandelier.

Percy flew up to the rafters with the chain, screwed in the hook, and the frame swung free. They stood back to admire it, just as the front door opened. Aunt Pitty Pat and Cousin Violet Mae, arms full of packages, stepped inside. The wind followed them in, and the rhinestone prisms tinkled merrily.

"Ohhhhhhhhh!" breathed Aunt Pitty Pat.

"Well," said Violet Mae, "it's about time that old thing was repaired."

15.

Kidnapped

Minabell leaned out of her bedroom window, watching the sun peep over Indian Mound Hill. It was going to be a prairie-perfect day.

She closed her eyes and took a deep breath. There was just the faintest scent of wild onion — now in full bloom across the state. She opened her eyes and watched the sun's rays slip down the Hill, across the park, and touch the statue of Geronimouse. One paw shaded his brow as he faced the rosy glow of the sunrise. The other paw held a flagpole on high. From its tip fluttered the Illinois state flag, its golden eagle proudly flying in the morning breeze.

"Oh, dear!" She had forgotten to lower the flag yesterday evening. It had been flying all night. Well, she thought, I won't need to raise it this morning. Just one less thing to do on this busy, happy day.

Aunt Pitty Pat's wish for a June wedding at Mousehaven Manor was coming true. Cousin Violet Mae was to be married on the first day of June, just one week away.

> "Tra la, tra la.
> Blackbird swinging
> On a cattail reed.
> Mousekin nibbling
> On a sunflower seed.
> Tra la, tra la!"

Humming to herself, Minabell closed the window and settled her tail-sling more firmly on her shoulder. There was much to be done before the ceremony. She buckled on her master keys and stepped out onto the balcony.

A faint cry came from one of the rooms. Aunt Pitty Pat slammed open the door of Violet Mae's bedroom, waving a piece of paper in the air. "VIOLET MAE! VIOLET MAE!"

Forgetting her arthritis, Aunt Pitty Pat ran down the grand staircase, tail flying out behind her. She rushed to the parlor, down the hall to the kitchen and back again, calling her niece.

"Aunty dear, wait. What's happened?" cried Minabell, catching up with her at the bottom of the stairs.

"Minabell," wailed Aunt Pitty Pat, "Violet Mae has been kidnapped — stolen away in the night." She collapsed onto a bench, clutching the paper.

Minabell sat next to her aunt and held her close. She suddenly knew — Count Von Flittermouse had struck again. In the midst of getting ready for the wedding, she had forgotten the vampire bat.

"Oh, mouseling! Violet Mae's bed wasn't slept in last night. I found this letter on her pillow. It's my fault. You tried to warn me. But I couldn't believe . . . he seemed such a well-mannered creature."

Minabell took the note from her aunt's trembling paw.

Ms. Minabell,
If you want Violet Mae back alive, come to the Oak Ridge Cemetery tonight at midnight. Bring the Magic Water.
Go directly to the entrance. My tomb is under the evergreen next to the wall. Come alone. You will be watched.
Death to the bride-to-be if you fail to bring the vial.

Count Von Flittermouse
The Shape-Changer

Aunt Pitty Pat stared into Minabell's eyes. "Mouseling . . . how could the Count get into the manor? Didn't you lock up last night?"

Minabell ran her paws over the keys hanging from her belt and tried to remember. She had bolted and padlocked the front and back doors. Then she had locked the windows, upstairs and down. "Yes, I . . ." Her paw touched the largest key on her belt — the dungeon key. And then she recalled the Count's words in the bell tower. *"A secret entrance, Ms. Mouse? How delightfully mysterious."*

They ran down the cellar stairs and raced under drying onions that were swaying from the ceiling. The padlock was dangling just as she had left it.

"Oh, Aunt Pitty Pat!" Minabell bent down, picked up Cousin Violet Mae's beaded purse, and silently handed it to her aunt.

16.

A Secret Plan

Aunt Pitty Pat gently smoothed Minabell's back fur. "Don't blame yourself. You tried to warn me."

Minabell stared into her aunt's eyes, wondering how to tell her.

"What is it, mouseling?"

Minabell swallowed hard and whispered, "I dropped the vial."

Aunt Pitty Pat took Minabell's paw and gave it an impatient little shake. "What are you saying?"

Minabell bowed her head. "The Count's note says Cousin Violet Mae will die unless

I bring him the Magic Water. But I don't have the water. It's gone."

"Where?" Aunt Pitty Pat jumped to her feet. "Come, mouseling. Show me."

They hurried through the root cellar and up the stairs to the great hall. Minabell led her aunt to the music room. As they drew near, their noses twitched at a faint scent. Minabell opened the door and they jumped back.

"Whiskers and tail feathers!" She couldn't believe her eyes.

"Land sakes! What happened to my little plant?" whispered Aunt Pitty Pat, staring into the room now filled with greenery.

Minabell stepped inside the room, ducked under the foliage, and ran to the hearth. She removed the carved box from its hiding place and hurried out to her aunt.

Pulling the vial out of the sand, she held it up to the light. "It's empty, Aunt Pitty Pat. The water drained out into the flower pot. I think the Magic Water from the Fountain of Youth must work on plants, too."

The tendrils and leaves were growing as Minabell and Aunt Pitty Pat watched — creeping inch by inch about the room. A huge, blue morning-glory bud unfolded, sending perfume sweet as a prairie breeze out into the hall.

Aunt Pitty Pat looked at the empty flask and then stared into the room again. She reread the ransom note, twitching her side-whiskers in thought. "Come," she said. "Bring the vial with you. There's more than one way to skin a snake."

Minabell replaced the box in the hearth. With a last look at the plant, she firmly closed the door and followed her wise little aunt down the hall to the kitchen.

❧

As the sun set in the west behind the manor, Minabell walked rapidly east toward Springfield, the state capital. Oak Ridge Cemetery was just outside this historic city. It was five mousemiles from Mousedale, and Minabell knew she must hurry if she was to arrive by midnight.

As she rounded the base of Indian Mound Hill, she happened to look up. Stars shimmered, tiny points of light in a darkening sky. And closer at hand, Madame Froganna's cave, perched on the top of the Hill, sent out a cozy glow. She and her family would be gathering around the soup kettle.

Minabell was sorely tempted to climb up to her friends' home. In her hurry, she had forgotten to eat dinner. She could do with a warm hug and a hot bowl of soup — and perhaps take Madame Froganna into her confidence.

Minabell hesitated for just a moment. No — that was not part of the plan she, Aunt Pitty Pat, and Percy had worked out. The Count had warned her to come alone. If she was to succeed in saving Cousin Violet Mae, the rescue must remain a secret.

She gave a final look upward at the circle of comforting light and started out across the prairie.

17.

Knock, Knock

Minabell pushed her way through the high grass, trying to find the turnoff — the seldom-used path to the city. Unseen thistle tugged at her back fur and scratched the tender skin on her nose and paws.

The moon, still low in the heavens, gave faint light, and Minabell almost missed the ancient wooden signpost. It was half hidden behind a large clover plant. The words SPRINGFIELD TRAIL were printed on the sign, and an arrow pointed to a narrow path through the grass.

She longed to turn on the flashlight she carried tucked into her belt-pouch. But she must not call attention to herself. The Count, the shape-changer, might be near. She half expected the wolf to appear on the path at any moment.

As she hurried along, her thoughts turned to her clever little aunt. Last night in the kitchen, Aunt Pitty Pat had filled the vial with plain Mousehaven water from the kitchen pump. A desperate plan, but the only one they had.

If the Count should waylay Minabell and steal the vial, he might not release Violet Mae. So they had decided that Percy would fly with the vial to the cemetery.

Percy was going to meet Minabell at the cemetery and hand over the water before she met the Count. They hoped the vampire wouldn't realize it was only prairie water — until it was too late. "Be ready to jump on board with your cousin," Percy had said. "I'll get us back to Mousehaven Manor as fast as a bat can fly."

"Which isn't very fast," Minabell muttered as she trudged along in the dark. Percy's way of flying — a diving, swooping movement — was meant for catching insects, not for speed.

Head down, Minabell concentrated on her footsteps and tried not to think of the cemetery meeting. She didn't notice that the trail was sloping downhill, or that the tall weeds on either side had been cut.

She was stopped abruptly by a gate lying across the path. It was built into a low stone fence that stretched right and left, cutting off further travel. She peered over the gate. The Sangamon River flowed gently in the moonlight.

On top of the stone wall, a large turtle was taking his ease, a green gate-keeper's cap on his head. He gazed down at Minabell and gave a friendly nod.

"Knock, knock," he said.

"Who's there?" replied Minabell.

"Hugo."

"Hugo who?"

"Hu — go's there?"

"It's Minabell Mouse. Please, sir, I need a ride across the river."

The turtle jumped nimbly off the wall and opened the gate. He took off his green cap and replaced it with a blue captain's cap. "Come aboard, miss," he said.

Minabell climbed up and settled herself on his back. The turtle waddled through the

gate, down to the river's edge, and slipped smoothly into the water. Five minutes later, he climbed up the opposite bank and deposited Minabell on the beach.

"Thank you, Captain Hugo," said Minabell, remembering her mousemanners.

"Aye, aye, miss," replied the captain. He disappeared back into the water.

Minabell turned her attention to the trail and searched the skies ahead. Stars blinked on and off like heavenly fireflies.

Far in the distance, the dome of the capitol blazed above the city of Springfield. Brightly lighted by spotlights, it was a beacon of hope for all Illinois creatures. Minabell hurried up the path.

18.

The Tomb

Minabell came to the end of Springfield Trail and stepped on a paved driveway. The surface was warm underfoot, still holding heat from the day. Ahead was the entrance to Oak Ridge Cemetery. She must hurry. It would soon be midnight.

She ran down the road, past a grassy hill, where gravestones marched across the closely cut lawn. On the top of the hill stood a pale stone building, its spire pointing to the stars — the Abraham Lincoln Memorial.

Minabell stopped to listen. Far away on the prairie, the tower bell at Mousehaven Manor was ringing. Twelve times it pealed, slow measured tones, tolling the hour of midnight. This was the signal agreed upon. Percy should be at the cemetery entrance waiting to hand over the vial.

Minabell ran off to the side of the road and slipped behind the petunias along the edge of the drive. Running under the plants, she arrived panting at the entrance.

Minabell peered out from under a low-hanging stem, its blossoms closed against the night air. The ransom note said the Count's tomb was under an evergreen. But which one? There were two evergreen bushes, standing like tall sentries, one on each side of the entrance. She removed the flashlight from her belt. Taking a deep breath, she stepped out into the moonlight.

She ran to the nearest evergreen and turned on the light. Nothing behind the bush, or under it. Minabell suddenly realized Percy should be there, waiting for her. "Percy, where are you?" she called softly. The only sound was the whispery lashing of the evergreens in the wind. She ran across the drive and searched behind the other bush.

The smell of worms, damp earth, and rotting things came from under the bottom branches. A mound of dirt, glistening with night dew, was piled up next to a large hole in the ground.

"Welcome, little mousie."

Minabell jumped back.

The flashlight slipped out of her trembling paw. She saw it roll toward the tomb's entrance and lunged after it. Minabell and the light disappeared down the hole.

She hit bottom with a thud, landing next to the flashlight. Its circle of light revealed dead insects, rolled up in sticky cobwebs, hanging from the ceiling. A shelf dug into the dirt wall held bottles of hair dye. Printed on the labels were the words:

LOVELY-LOCKS

*

LANOLIN ENRICHED
TINT NO. 106

Heavy breathing and a familiar shuffling sound came from the shadows on her right. Minabell scrambled to her feet and beamed the flashlight into the corner.

The vampire, Count Von Flittermouse, leaned on a cane and squinted into the light. "Turn it off," he croaked, throwing a withered wing up to shield his eyes. Minabell turned the light aside. The Count limped over to his coffin and put on the sunglasses that were lying on the lid. "Ahh," he said, tipping his high hat. "So nice to see you, my dear."

Minabell stared at the Count, hardly recognizing him. His scrawny frame was bent almost double as he wobbled toward her on shaking legs. All his fur had fallen out, except for a few tufts growing out of his ears. He seemed not to have realized this — for he had doused himself with LOVELY-LOCKS hair dye. The leathery skin on his wings and body was streaked with brown splashes of Tint No. 106.

The Count ogled her, smacking his thin

lips. Minabell suddenly noticed the tiny skulls and bones scattered about the cave. She shivered. "Where is Violet Mae?"

The Count ignored her question. He raised his cane and poked her sharply in the ribs. "GIVE ME THE MAGIC WATER!" he screamed. "Hurry! I have no time to lose." Drool hung from his mouth, and his eyes rolled up in his head.

Minabell backed up. "Please, sir — I don't have it. Percy has the vial."

The Count stopped drooling and rolled his eyes back into place. He gave her a hard level stare. "LIES! I searched him."

"What? You've seen Percy?"

Instead of answering, the Count flung himself at Minabell and grabbed her pouch. Tearing it from her belt, he tripped and fell. He ripped open the pouch. It was empty except for two silver pebbles that rolled onto the floor. "Where is the vial?" the vampire whispered, struggling to stand. He fell back weakly, staring up at her.

A heavy silence filled the tomb.

"Hic."

Minabell whirled around. She would know that voice — that dear voice — anywhere. She searched the dark corners. "PERCY! Where are you?"

"Hic, hic."

The voice was coming from the coffin. She ran and tugged at the lid. It was stuck. Minabell snatched the Count's cane from the ground and used it as a lever. The lid came off with a pop, clattering to the floor. Minabell stared down at Percy and Cousin Violet Mae. Bound and gagged, they lay side by side in the casket.

She ripped off Percy's gag and bindings. He lifted a wing and silently pointed. "The vial," he whispered.

They quickly helped Cousin Violet Mae out of the casket. She gazed at them with tear-filled eyes, for once speechless. Suddenly she gave a terrified squeal and pointed behind Minabell.

A huge spider was galloping toward them on four pairs of hairy legs. Holding onto his high hat, he skidded to a stop. The creature loomed over them, body bristles vibrating. His eight round eyes glared down at them. Minabell could see herself and Percy reflected in the two center eyes, big as Aunt Pitty Pat's dinner plates.

The black fangs hung down from each side of his mouth like a giant scissors. They snipped and sliced the air — mouseinches from their heads.

"It's the shape-changer, Count Von Flittermouse," whispered Percy, pulling Minabell back. He removed the vial from under his wing and started to hand it to her. The spider snatched the vial in midair and raised it triumphantly to his mouth. He noisily sucked in the water. Crushing the flask with his fangs, he dropped the broken glass at their feet.

The spider reared up, waving his front legs in the air, and gave a victor's cry. The howl of a prairie wolf filled the tomb.

We must get out, thought Minabell. But it was too late.

The spider knocked Minabell to the ground with one blow of his leg and held her down with a heavy claw. The weight was so great on her chest, she could hardly breathe.

Percy started toward her. "No!" she gasped. "Save Violet Mae."

As Percy ran to the entrance with Violet Mae, the spider bent over Minabell. Grinding his fangs, the creature's ugly head filled her vision. Minabell, heart pounding, closed her eyes and held her breath.

The creature suddenly stiffened. Minabell's eyes flew open. The spider started trembling, thrashing his huge head back and forth, the fangs brushing her breast fur. His high hat tumbled to the floor.

He staggered and fell backward — releasing Minabell. She could breathe again. Coughing, she jumped to her feet. The spider lay on his back, twitching and jerking his legs in the air. As she watched, the light went out of his eight eyes, and his legs collapsed on his stomach. With much groaning, stretching of skin, and popping of bones, the spider changed back into the bat.

"Hurry, Minabell," urged Percy.

The ancient vampire staggered toward her, crooning, "Mousie, mousie, mou . . ." Minabell stared at him, unable to move.

Slowly, slowly, the Count's body turned in a half-circle. He reached out with a claw and caught hold of her leg. The evil little eyes were suddenly filled with fury. He had guessed about the Magic Water.

The Count's breath escaped in a long drawn-out hiss. He relaxed his hold on her leg, and his claw dropped away. Covering his head with a wing, he sank to the ground.

Minabell grabbed the flashlight. She hesitated — then snatched up the vampire's sunglasses and dashed for the entrance. As Percy flew out into the night, Minabell beamed the light back inside the tomb.

A small heap of body-dust was all that remained of Count Von Flittermouse.

Ms. Pitty Pat Mouse
requests the honor of your presence
at the wedding of her niece
Violet Mae
to
Mr. Rhinestone Rodent

DATE: June first
PLACE: Mousehaven Manor
Mousedale, Illinois

Party and refreshments following
R.S.V.P.

19.

Big Doings
at Mousehaven Manor

The prairie sun arose on a perfect wedding day, not a cloud in the sky. The ceremony, and the party following, were being held at Geronimouse Park in front of the manor. The popular Rodent Rhythm Boys had been engaged to provide music for the celebration.

A billowing silk tent was set up, large enough to hold all the guests. Every creature in Mousedale, from the youngest mouseling-in-arms to the eldest graybeard, had been invited. And all had accepted, for Rhinestone Rodent was everyone's favorite.

As Rhinestone had promised, he was dressed, to Violet Mae's complete satisfaction, in a new costume. From the top of his wide-brimmed Western hat to his high-heeled Western boots, he was outfitted in white — all encrusted with swirls of purple rhinestones.

The bride wore a lavender chiffon veil, its long train floating out behind her. It was held in place by a floral crown of Queen Anne's lace. In her paws she carried a bouquet of violets. Tiny gold and white butterflies fluttered about her head, attracted by her flower headdress.

Parson Owl flew in for the ceremony. Percy gave the bride away. He was wearing new sunglasses. They were the glasses Minabell had picked up at the crypt. Since the Count would not be needing them anymore, she had given them to Percy.

Minabell, of course, was the maid of honor. To cover her sore tail, she tied a pink bow over the bare spot where the fur was missing.

And in the bell tower, the Bat family was kept busy ringing the bell, a joyous announcement to the countryside that a wedding was in progress.

After the ceremony, light refreshments were served under the bridal tent. There was a salad of black-eyed Susans and wild onions tossed with a sweet-and-sour milkweed dressing; heart-shaped sandwiches filled with three different mouth-watering fillings — minced buttercup jelly, crushed beebalms, and creamed clover; and, of course, the wedding cake.

The youngest rodents were only interested in the desserts. Heaping cones of frozen pokeberry and mayapple ices were handed out to the bright-eyed youngsters as fast as they could be made.

"Praise the prairie skies, Minabell!" cried Aunt Pitty Pat as one of the frog children leapt over her head. All around them the tads were excitedly leapfrogging about as they licked their ice cones.

Aunt Pitty Pat laughed. "If the little ones are here, can Madame Froganna be far behind?"

Sure enough, Madame had set up a booth near the tent and was busy telling fortunes. Minabell wasn't surprised to see Frogella, sitting on top of her mother's head, counting the cash. Madame glanced up, saw Minabell, and winked.

On the largest table in the tent stood a fountain of Aunt Pitty Pat's prizewinning dandelion wine overflowing a statue, carved in ice, of Geronimouse. This display was the center of attention as the guests toasted themselves and the happy couple.

There was a sudden musical flourish and a roll of drums. Rhinestone stepped forward, took Violet Mae by the paw, and led her to the bandstand. He strummed his guitar, gazing at his bride with adoring eyes. Violet Mae lifted her pink nose in the air, and they began singing a duet in two-part harmony.

"Lavender's blue
Dilly, dilly
Lavender's green.
When I am king

Dilly, dilly
You shall be queen.

"Who told you so
Dilly, dilly?
Who told you so?

" 'Twas my heart told me so
Dilly, dilly.
'Twas my heart told me so."

Amid happy laughter and applause, the newlyweds stepped down from the bandstand and led the guests back to the tent, where the three-tiered wedding cake was now on display.

Aunt Pitty Pat had baked the cake herself. It stood thirty-six mouseinches high, covered with pink icing and decorated with spun-sugar forget-me-nots. On the very top stood two little candy mice, holding paws and gazing into each other's candy eyes.

Minabell did the honors, cutting a large piece of cake for everyone. Then she and her aunt wrapped slices of cake in lavender napkins for the guests to take home — a remembrance of one of Mousehaven Manor's best parties ever.

∽

As the sun set behind Mousehaven Manor, Aunt Pitty Pat, Minabell, and Percy Bat stood on the manor's front steps, waving farewell to the newlyweds. Mr. and Mrs. Rhinestone Rodent were flying away on their honeymoon.

"Good-bye, good-bye," they called from the back of the gaily decorated prairie hawk. With a loud squawk, the bird flew over the park, his lavender and white tail-ribbons streaming out behind him. Cousin Violet Mae threw her bridal bouquet down to Minabell. It drifted to earth, twirling slowly on the evening breeze, and landed — on Percy's head.

The prairie hawk caught an updraft, and the happy couple floated out of sight over the rim of Indian Mound Hill.

20.

The Morning-glory Room

It was November, just five months since the wedding. Snowflakes drifted silently down, heaping up on the windowsill, like bits of dandelion fluff.

Minabell wiped the moisture from the window and stared out. "Company is coming, Aunt Pitty Pat."

Her aunt jumped up from her rocker and ran to look. She searched the evening sky and saw a small bird flying rapidly toward the manor. "Land sakes, Minabell! It's Gaylord Cardinal."

"Oh, Aunt Pitty Pat! Maybe he has a

letter from Cousin Violet Mae and Rhine-stone. But — " Minabell looked doubtful. "Are you sure it's Gaylord?"

Her aunt's eyes twinkled, and her side-whiskers twitched with excitement. "Oh yes, mouseling! Small birds have a special way of flying. They must flap their wings very fast to stay airborne. And Gaylord is carrying his mailbag over his wing. This makes him appear heavier on one side."

Minabell and her aunt watched the mail-bird approach the manor. "Poor Gaylord," said Aunt Pitty Pat. "It must be hard to fly in this weather."

They were in the music room, renamed the *morning-glory room* in honor of the giant flower overflowing its pot. The plant filled the entire room. The curling tendrils, thick with heart-shaped leaves, tumbled off the stand, grew up the walls, and covered the ceiling. Blue and white bell-shaped flowers, large as Minabell's head, hung from the rafters.

Studying the sky over Indian Mound Hill,

Minabell announced, "You're right, Aunt Pitty Pat. It's Gaylord Cardinal."

They hurried outside and stood shivering on the front steps, peering through the falling snow. A flash of red against the white, and the cardinal fluttered to earth, exhausted and panting.

"Do come in, Gaylord," urged Aunt Pitty Pat, leading the mailbird up the stairs and into the manor.

Flapping his wings to remove the snow, Gaylord hurried across the great hall to the morning-glory room. He took a deep breath of the perfumed air, raised his headcrest, and fanned it out with a happy sigh. He dropped his mailbag and sat down on one of the gilt chairs. "This room grows more beautiful every time I visit," he said.

Aunt Pitty Pat poured him a cup of her special tonic drink. "Ahhh!" Gaylord breathed in the sweet aroma floating up from the steaming cup. "You brew the finest tea in the state of Illinois, Aunt Pitty Pat."

The tea, made from the crushed leaves of

the morning-glory plant, had magical healing powers. Creatures came to the manor from all over the prairie to sip the drink and cure their ills. Thanks to this tonic, Aunt Pitty Pat had regained her health. Her arthritis had disappeared, and her beautiful side-whiskers were, once again, a golden brown. Minabell, too, showed the good effects of the drink. The fur had grown back on her tail, and her coat was soft and shining.

After several cups, Gaylord was ready to brave the snowstorm again. He jumped to his claws, picked up his mailbag, and headed for the door. "Oops!" He skidded to a stop, rummaged in his bag, and produced a letter addressed to Ms. Minabell Mouse and Ms. Pitty Pat Mouse.

After seeing Gaylord on his way, Minabell locked the front door and rejoined her aunt in their new sitting room. They sat in their rockers, surrounded by the greenery, and sipped their tea while Minabell read the letter out loud.

Dear Cousin and Aunty,

Greetings from Texas. We have found a cozy nest near the theater where Rhinestone is the star attraction.

But the big news is that we are the proud parents of twins — Baby Violet Mae and Baby Rhinestone, Jr.

They are beautiful babies, taking after their mother and father, of course. But you can judge for yourselves. We will be coming home to Mousehaven Manor for Thanksgiving.

Lovingly yours,

Violet Mae

Aunt Pitty Pat clapped her paws. "Praise the prairie skies — Violet Mae is a mother! Imagine that!"

"Imagine being a great-aunt," said Minabell fondly. "Congratulations, *Great*-Aunt Pitty Pat."

About the Author and the Illustrator

Mary DeBall Kwitz is the author and/or illustrator of more than a dozen books, including *Little Chick's Story*; *Rabbit's Search for a Little House*; and *Gumshoe Goose, Private Eye*. Her first book for Scholastic Hardcover was *Shadow Over Mousehaven Manor*. She lives in Port Charlotte, Florida.

Stella Ormai was the 1980 recipient of the Don Freeman Memorial Grant from the Society of Children's Book Writers. She illustrated *Heartbeats: Your Body, Your Heart* (a 1983 Outstanding Science Trade Book for Children); and *Shadow Over Mousehaven Manor* and *I Am Leaper* for Scholastic Hardcover. She lives with her husband and daughter in Providence, Rhode Island.

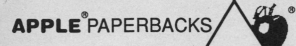

Frankenstein Doesn't Plant Petunias
Ghosts Don't Eat Potato Chips
and
Aliens Don't Wear Braces
...or do they?

Find out about the creepiest, weirdest, funniest things that happen to the Bailey School Kids!

Collect and read them all!

❏ BAS47070-1	Aliens Don't Wear Braces	$2.75
❏ BAS47071-X	Frankenstein Doesn't Plant Petunias	$2.75
❏ BAS45854-X	Ghosts Don't Eat Potato Chips	$2.75
❏ BAS44822-6	Leprechauns Don't Play Basketball	$2.75
❏ BAS44477-8	Santa Claus Doesn't Mop Floors	$2.75
❏ BAS43411-X	Vampires Don't Wear Polka Dots	$2.75
❏ BAS44061-6	Werewolves Don't Go To Summer Camp	$2.50

Available wherever you buy books, or use this order form.